This edition published by Parragon Books Ltd in 2016

Parragon Books Ltd
Chartist House
15–17 Trim Street
Bath BA1 1HA, UK
www.parragon.com

Adapted from the original story by Thomas Macri
Illustrated by Luke Ross and Dean White

ISBN 978-1-4748-3602-9

Printed in China

Bath · New York · Cologne · Melbourne · Delhi
Hong Kong · Shenzhen · Singapore

A world filled with ideas, hope and potential will always attract a great many villains. But for every villain that attacks, there is a hero to defeat them. This is the story of a team of those mighty heroes known as ... the Avengers.

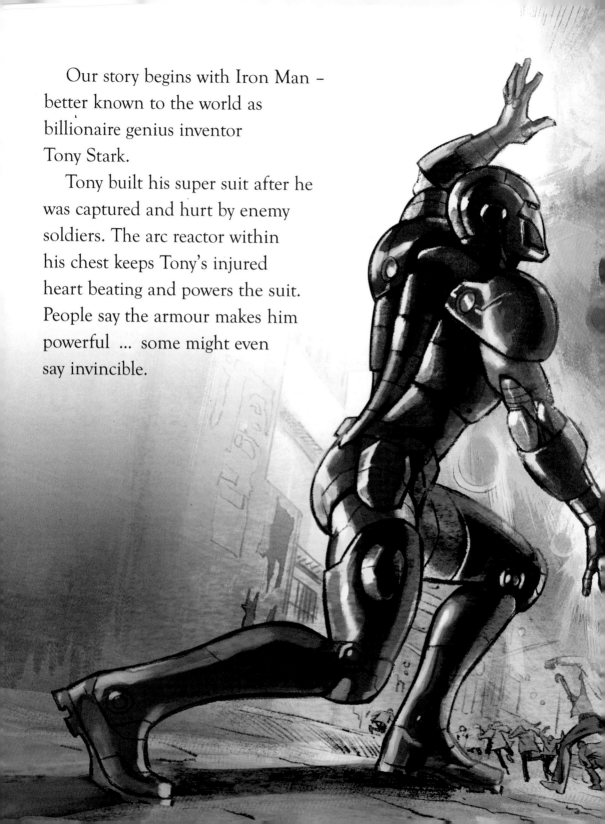

Our story begins with Iron Man –
better known to the world as
billionaire genius inventor
Tony Stark.

Tony built his super suit after he
was captured and hurt by enemy
soldiers. The arc reactor within
his chest keeps Tony's injured
heart beating and powers the suit.
People say the armour makes him
powerful ... some might even
say invincible.

It wasn't long before Tony found another hero to work with. Natasha Romanoff spent years training to be a top secret spy, handling only the most dangerous and daring missions. Eventually, Natasha was recruited by a secret spy organisation called S.H.I.E.L.D., where she was given the code name ... Black Widow.

And Black Widow brought another hero to Tony's team – her friend, Hawkeye.

Orphaned at an early age, Clint Barton worked for a travelling circus as a master archer. After witnessing Iron Man rescue people in danger, Clint knew that he, too, wanted to be a Super Hero and help those in need. Clint made a costume and created a variety of trick arrows, equipped with exploding tips, stunners and electrical nets. That's when Clint became Hawkeye. But when Hawkeye's arrows didn't cut it, there was always ...

... The Incredible Hulk! Hulk came into being when scientist Bruce Banner was exposed to gamma radiation during an experiment. Whenever he got angry, Banner transformed into a huge green hero with super strength.

But the Hulk was big ... and scary. People were afraid of him. No matter how much he tried to help, people just didn't trust him. So although he wanted to help protect the planet from evil, the Hulk mostly kept to himself.

Although these four heroes worked well together, they weren't a complete team just yet. They were still missing something....

Far away, in another realm, a demi-god called Thor was battling his brother, Loki. Loki wanted to rule Thor's kingdom, Asgard. Thor imprisoned his brother in a place called the Isle of Silence. This made Loki very angry. He wanted revenge! So he used his powers to search the Earth – a place his brother had sworn to protect – to find someone people feared and distrusted. Most importantly, it had to be someone who could defeat Thor.

He soon found someone – the Incredible Hulk! Loki used his powers of mischief to trick the Hulk into thinking that a broken rail was about to cause a high-speed train to crash. The Hulk stopped the train, thinking he had saved the day.

But the broken rail was just an illusion! The people on the train thought the Hulk was trying to hurt them. Word spread fast that the Hulk was on a rampage. It was up to Iron Man, Black Widow and Hawkeye to stop him.

But just as the three
heroes cornered the Hulk,
Thor captured his brother and
exposed him as the true villain.
Thor banished Loki to Asgard,
where he would face justice far away
from Earth.

The five heroes liked working
together. They realised that, as
individuals, they were just Super
Heroes – but as a team, they were
mighty. And so they became ...
the Avengers!

These five heroes made a powerful team. But something
was about to happen that would change that team forever.
After battling Namor, Prince of Atlantis, the Avengers were
cruising through the Arctic Circle in their submarine. Suddenly, they
spotted something strange in a block of ice floating nearby!
The Hulk swam out to the ice and took it back to the sub.
Iron Man slowly thawed the ice to reveal ...

... Captain America, the famous
Super-Soldier from World War II!

Cap had saved the world from
the criminal organization Hydra
and its leader, Red Skull. But after
a freak accident, he had been left
frozen in ice for decades. Confused
and on guard, Cap listened to
the Avengers explain what had
happened to him. But before the
group could get too friendly,
the sub shook.

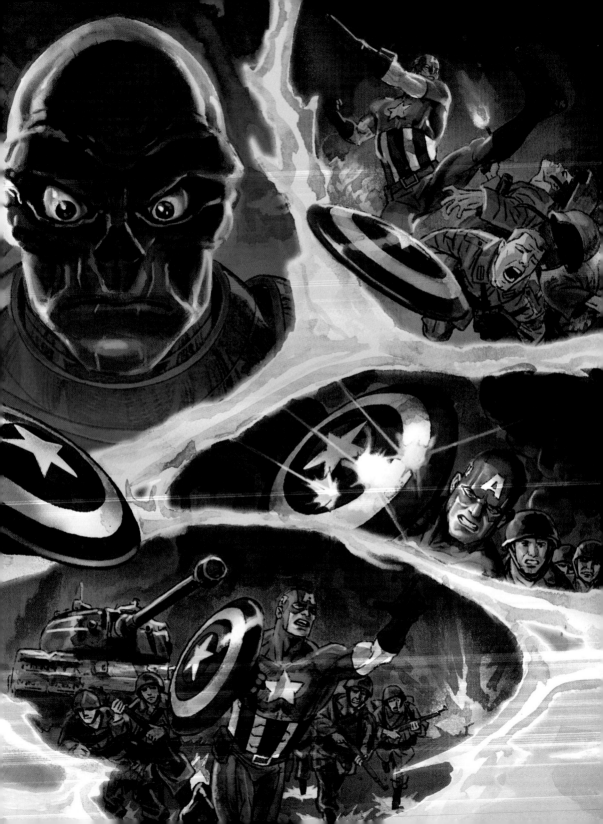

Namor was back, and he'd brought an army of
Atlanteans with him! The Avengers, with the
help of Captain America, drove off Namor and
his army. They had combined their forces
and stopped him from waging war on the
surface world.

With Cap on board, the Avengers
felt their team was finally complete.
Captain America raised his shield
and the others rallied
around him.

A new team had been born: Iron Man, Black Widow, Hawkeye, Hulk, Thor and now Captain America. The villains of the world were up against something special – something mighty! And if ever a threat were to arise that was too big for one hero ... the Avengers would assemble!